SHROPSHIRE
GHOST STORIES

Retold by

SALLY TONGE

First published in 2007 by Sutton Publishing

Reprinted in 2008 by
The History Press
The Mill, Brimscombe Port,
Stroud, Gloucestershire, GL5 2QG
www.thehistorypress.co.uk

Reprinted 2009, 2010

Copyright © Sally Tonge, 2007

All rights reserved. No part of this publication may be reproduced, stored in a retrieval system, or transmitted, in any form, or by any means, electronic, mechanical, photocopying, recording or otherwise, without the prior permission of the publisher and copyright holder.

Sally Tonge hereby asserts the moral right to be identified as the author of this work.

British Library Cataloguing in Publication Data
A catalogue record for this book is available from the British Library.

ISBN 978-07509-4510-3

Typeset in 12/16 pt Garamond.
Printed and bound in England.

Contents

Acknowledgements 5
Introduction 7

BOTTLED GHOSTS	9	THE DEVIL	53
The Bagbury Bull	10	Slashrags & the Devil	54
		Will o' the Wisp	59
WHITE LADIES & HEADLESS GHOSTS	13	OTHER MALIGN & MAGICAL CREATURES	63
The White Lady of Longnor	14	The Legend of Ogo's Hole	64
Brave Tommy & the Ghost	18	The Welsh Brownie	68
		The Gorsty Bank Bogies	69
VENGEFUL SPIRITS	22		
For the Love of Horses	23	HEROES	72
Squire Blount	28	Wild Edric	73
The Deeds & Nasty End of Judge Leighton	31	WATER	77
		The Asrai	78
CHILDREN	35	The Nicky Nicky Nye	81
The Tale of Sarah Hoggins	36		
Madam Pigott	38	STORIES OF OUR TIMES	88
		The Fires of Wem	89
MURDERS	42		
Bloody Jack of Shrewsbury	43	GRAVEYARDS	92
		The Phantom Funeral at Ratlinghope	93
INDELIBLE BLOODSTAINS	48		
The Bloodstain at Condover Hall	49		

Bibliography 96

Acknowledgements

This project has been a long while in the creation. Thanks to Helen Sample and Gordon Dickens who first approached me with the idea. Thanks to Shropshire Library Services and to the Records and Research Department for access to books, pamphlets, journals and guidance. Jimmy Eccles and Des Quarrell read the manuscript at various stages and offered valuable feedback. Fran O'Boyle produced wonderful illustrations and Philip Jones provided the photographic images. Time to work on this project was made possible with a grant from the Arts Council, West Midlands. Audiences in schools, village halls, pubs and storytelling clubs have listened to these stories as I have told and shaped them, guided by their reactions and responses. Friends have supported and listened as I have worked through this. Thanks to Elsie Rowson for her time to share stories over a cup of tea. Lara Sproson proof read with an eagle eye. Maxine Hall is a valued childcarer and technical witch and Brian Carrington has helped me interpret the material for further telling in song. Seamus and Ruairi have been my support, inspiration and a delightful, vital distraction. Thanks and love to you all.

Introduction

The language of stories is full of words relating to fabric: you spin a good yarn, weave the plot, embroider the truth, and sometimes lose your thread in a story. Stories are a patchwork of fact and invention; patches borrowed from here and there and sewn together to create a tale that will keep the listener rapt by the telling and wrapped up in a world of imagination. Once a story is worn out, then a new storyteller picks out the worn out fragment, replaces it with a patch borrowed from somewhere else and breathes new life into it.

In the same way, this book is a collection of stories which have been told and shaped not by historical fact but by human voices and minds; continually weaving and sewing together stories, inaccuracies, imaginings and fantasies. For as long as humans have been able to communicate, we have told stories to each other. We are all storytellers; we all tell tales of our lives, our past, what happened yesterday, and the tales get amplified with retelling.

Just as a patchwork quilt was once other items of clothing and fabric, so stories have their origins somewhere else, but it's so long ago that those origins are long forgotten – and do those origins really matter? A patchwork quilt can keep you warm no matter what it's made of and a good story needs to be heard no matter how it came to be!

Wherever you go, people will have a ghostly story which they want to share with you, a room that they don't feel comfortable in, an encounter with a dead person, poltergeist activity or just inexplicable happenings. In a way, it's not the story that they tell that is important, it is our urge to tell them.

Much research has been done, employing scientific techniques as well as some older methods to document and explore the ghostliness of places. Indeed, people can go on ghost walks in town and country locations and visit sites where ghostly activity has been detected. Books have been produced which catalogue ghost stories area by area; they explore some of the background to these sightings and the impact they have on the people who have witnessed these things.

As a professional storyteller, I am fascinated with our urge to tell stories; the desire to have a tale to tell on a dark night or around a camp-fire, on a long journey or simply in response to a child's request. No matter how advanced our technological world becomes, connections of voice, audience and story will always have a power.

A lot of this material is wispy, hard to place in a date, time or space. Some of the stories in this book are told the world over; parallel stories can be found in other counties of Britain and have through time been attributed to Shropshire. There are common motifs such as white ladies, ghosts in bottles, the Devil's antics and hero legends.

When information is scarce or confused, storytellers use invention – we make it up! Where we think the plot runs a bit thin, then we add a bit extra. If our listeners are enjoying a gruesome part of the story, then we may well embellish and add extra bits.

A lot of approaches to ghost stories have been rather historical and located in a framework of fact – relating to place, teller and time. This book is unashamedly a storyteller's approach to the material: the stories are the product of years and years of retelling, borrowing, anachronism and creation.

This is not an audit of Shropshire ghost stories, other books have done that excellently, and neither have I attempted to retell stories with a countywide spread.

These are stories I enjoy telling, full of the flavours of a good ghostly yarn with bits begged, borrowed and stolen from the world of narratives that surround us. Ultimately they are for you, the reader, to recall, retell, add bits and move to locations you know.

They are a gift. A story is the only present you can give away and still keep yourself! Be generous, tell them on!

Sally Tonge
Candlemas 2007

BOTTLED GHOSTS

Bottling a ghost is one way of tidying them up. It's similar to the idea of a genie in a lamp; imprisoned and waiting for the right person to come and free them. Many popular stories tell of the gifts, justice and good fortune that these newly freed spirits bring. There are a few very disgruntled spirits bottled up in Shropshire who would bring different gifts should they ever get free! An interesting detail is that the bottle should always be dark or opaque, so that the spirit can't see out. There are other stories in this collection that see their ghosts ending up in bottles.

The Bagbury Bull

There was once an evil old man who was the squire at Bagbury near Hyssington in the south-west of Shropshire. Local lore tells that in all his life he only ever did two good deeds. He once gave bread and cheese to a starving child (although the bread was stale and the cheese was mouldy) and another time he gave his waistcoat to a beggar man (it was a hot day and the squire was glad to be rid of the extravagantly embroidered garment).

He made people's lives a misery with his mean and money-grabbing ways. A few locals sought the help of a local hen-wife, a witch, and asked her to make a charm to rid them of the old man forever. The old crone thought long and hard about their request and twiddled the long curly whiskers on her bony chin as she rocked in her chair in front of the fire and leafed through her recipe books.

After many weeks of thought, locked in her cottage deep in the woods, the old hag one day shuffled into the village and presented a powder, wrapped in a large leaf and bound with a string of flax. She declared that this was the spell that would ensure the miserable old squire never got peace in this life or the next. The villagers were happy with the prospect of his eternal torment and the powder was passed to a serving girl at the squire's house. She managed to slip the grains into the old man's wine.

The villagers endured the remaining years of the miserable old squire's life, consoled by the fact that his punishment awaited him beyond the grave.

Eventually the squire died but the witch's potion backfired somewhat. For the squire's spirit took on the form of a monstrous, bellowing, snorting bull

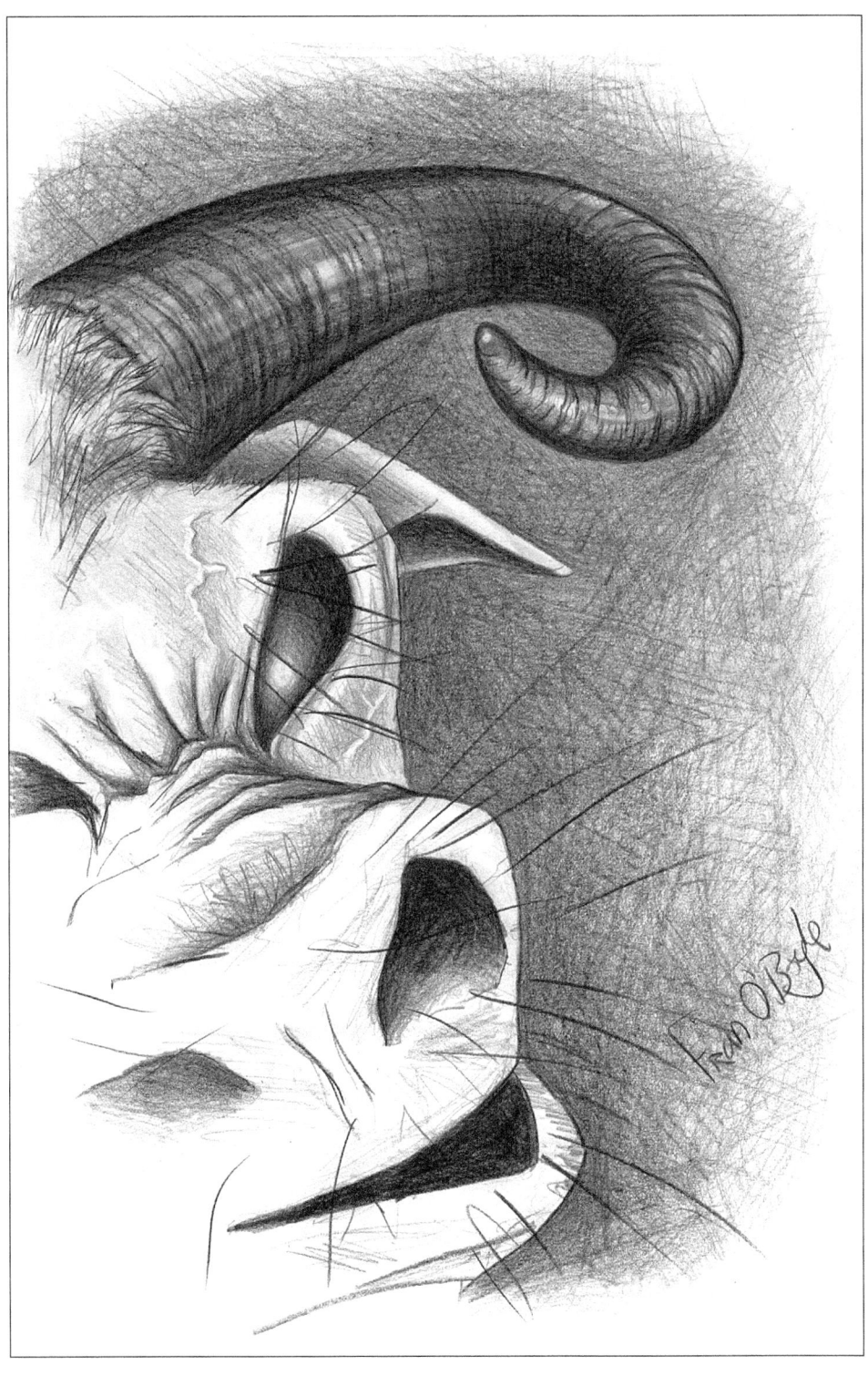

that would stamp about the lanes, trample the crops and terrorise the villagers night after night. The eternal torment, it seemed, was to be theirs and not his!

The local parson decided that enough was enough and an exorcism had to be performed to lay the ghost to rest. The entire village and a team of parsons rounded up the ferocious beast and led it to the church at Hyssington. The parson stood in the pulpit and led the incantations of psalms and prayers above the roars of the bull as it careered and kicked about the church.

Another parson joined in. The first shadows of night played on the whitewashed walls of the church and the bull began to visibly shrink before the eyes of the astonished villagers and the earnest clergy, it was overpowered by the words of the good book.

As night fell around them, candles were lit to keep the powers of darkness at bay as the exorcism continued. Presently the bull was no bigger than a dog but inexhaustibly bucking and snorting around.

All at once, the little bull managed one mighty howling bellow and snuffed out every single candle. The congregation was plunged into darkness. In the darkness, the doorway to the evil world had been opened and the bull began to grow rapidly and crazily, beyond its original size, until it filled the entire church. So huge, fat and strong was the spirit that it caused the roof timbers to groan and the stonework cracked with the pressure of his huge body.

It just so happened that one of the parsons was blind. He didn't need a candle to read the scriptures as he knew them by heart, and he carried on reciting, despite the bull's furious roars that practically drowned out his voice. A single candle was relit and the parson's persistent prayers combined with the glimmer of light were enough to diminish the forces of evil once more. On and on prayed the blind parson and again the bull began to shrink, to the size of an elephant, then a horse, then a dog, a cat and then finally a mouse.

The miniature bull was scooped up and placed into one of the bystander's boots. This was tightly laced up and buried deep under the weathered threshold step of the church.

A builder was recently asked to install a ramp for disabled access into the church and was under strict instructions not to disturb the slab on the step. He was careful to obey!

It is said that until more recent work on the church was carried out, the cracks from where the enormous spectral bull strained against the walls were visible.

WHITE LADIES & HEADLESS GHOSTS

A common ghostly vision is the drifting white form, bedazzling and translucent. Shropshire has plenty of White Ladies. The White Lady of Hale near Titterstone Clee emerges at night and, wringing her hands, goes to the place where she witnessed her son, Richard, being murdered. All that remains is a bloodstain on the floor which she anxiously paces around. There was a Grey Lady at Badger Hall who would appear at Christmas dances. She would try to speak to stunned dancers there, pleading and begging, in dreamlike torment. The discovery of a jewellery box seemed to appease her and she can now rest.

Bridgnorth boasts a Black Lady too. This tragic character haunts a building at the bottom of the Cartway. If you peer into the garden of what is now a bar, there are two busts of a little boy and girl there. Long ago these children were playing hide and seek in the cellar of the house. As they hid and waited, a sudden flood warning was given when the River Severn burst its banks. The mother thought the children had run on ahead with their father and so she locked the house and raced up the Cartway to escape the rising tide. She was mistaken. The children were still playing their game when the water began to pour in through the cellar window. They made their way up the cellar steps but were too small to reach the door handle and there they perished. By the time the mother discovered that her children were missing, it was too late. Two statues were carved to the children's memory and the poor grief-stricken ghost of a mother replays her frantic search in her black shadowy form on dark nights up and down the Cartway.

The White Lady of Longnor

Along the road to Leebotwood there is a pool, known locally as Black Pool. It is said to be bottomless; generations of parents have warned their children of the dangers of skating and sliding upon it in the frozen winter.

There was once a beautiful young woman who lived at Longnor. On a crisp, bright winter's day, she chose to ignore the warnings of her mother. She took her skates and stole off down to the pool to join her boyfriend to dance and skate beneath the blue sky and the icy winter sunshine.

They were young and in love and they were going to live forever. We have all had that thought, haven't we? They twirled and danced together; hearts warmed by love and faces hot from kisses. Suddenly, there was an echoing crack. Instantly a fault line in the ice shot across the pond. A narrow hole opened up directly under the girl's feet. Down she fell, straight out of the arms of her lover, and into the water below.

The young man tried in vain to reach his girl, smashing at the ice with his skates. Then he lay flat on his belly, reaching his arms through the ice hole trying to grasp her. Finally, a face floated up and appeared through the thick ice window. They exchanged one last chill kiss through the glaze before she sank down for a last time, leaving the boy weeping with ice melting on his lips.

It was said that her ghost would rise up from the pool and wander through the village and on cold nights she would whisper warnings through children's windows and locks not to go skating on the pond. You would feel a sudden, thin draught of air cut across the room and that would be her.

Many years later, there was a young man called Hughes who told how he was out poaching in the full moon. He came to cross the narrow bridge at Longnor Brook when he saw a young woman approaching the other end. In the moonlight, she looked so beautiful and he decided to sneak up and play a trick on her. He slunk back and hid in the shadows. Hearing her light tread on the bridge, he jumped out and went to clasp his arms around her waist to steal a kiss! His arms clasped around . . . nothing . . . thin air! The ghost of the young girl walked right through him and continued on her way. The young man hurried to the pub where his gibbering shock was enough to convince listeners there that he had been properly spooked.

Some time afterwards there was a village dance. In a place where everybody knew everybody, these were simple matchmaking occasions, with rumour-mongers and gossips at the ready to stir up scandal in a moment.

So there was a great buzz of excitement that night when a stranger turned up to dance. She had a bewitching beauty, mysterious elegance and was dressed all in white. She joined in but would only dance in a ring and never be held for a partner dance.

She entranced everybody on that night including a fellow called Jack. He was usually one of those who hugged the fringes of the dance floor like a nervous child clings to its mother's skirts. He was so clumsy and heavy-footed. Yet, on that night, he was compelled to step out onto the floor and danced at the stranger's side all night long. He amazed himself with the lightness and rhythm that he found in his feet. Each move and turn that his neighbour made seemed to spin out a web tangling round Jack and binding him up in her bewitchment until, at midnight, she slipped away as quietly as she had arrived.

When she left, Jack could do nothing else but follow her, it was as if he was being dragged by a strong invisible thread. Wide-eyed and gaping-mouthed, he followed the woman as she walked along the lane and far from the lights of the dance.

With Jack still trailing behind, she picked up a path across the field towards the pond. Jack's arms were stretched out in front of him and he begged, 'Just one kiss, just one kiss', as he helplessly followed like a sleepwalker.

At Black Pool's edge she didn't hesitate for a moment but continued into the water. Her dress swirled around as she faded from view, enveloped by the water lapping round her waist, her chest, her neck, her head until she completely disappeared.

Jack trailed into the water behind her, and suddenly let out a shriek as he came to his senses. It was so cold! The spell was broken and he found himself waist-deep in freezing pond water.

Standing dumbstruck, his arms foolishly embracing his own shaking shoulders, the young man realised that he had been charmed by the White Lady of Longnor. She stalks about on chill nights, entrancing young men and inviting them to dance with her, on the thin ice of the heart.

Brave Tommy & the Ghost

A long time ago, there was a house in Ludlow that was said to be so haunted that people wouldn't dare visit it. The spirit of a restless old man prowled round one of the bedrooms, sighing and moaning, moving pictures and furniture, rattling door-knobs, testing the window catches and giving the family no peace at all. People had long ago given up trying to sleep in that room. Even passers-by would hasten their steps and keep their heads down, not daring even to glance up at the one dark, cobwebby window.

On the advice of some friends, the family invited the services of a man known simply as Tommy to help rid them of the ghost. Nobody knew much about Tommy, except that he was a simple living man who lived quietly on the edge of the town, who knew about the ways of ghosts and the 'other world'.

Tommy agreed to come and sit the night with the ghost and do what he could. All he asked was that he should be left alone in the room with a bottle of good beer.

It was an icy winter's night when Tommy was shown into the room. A table was set with the ale he'd requested and a chair was pulled up close to a roaring fire. He rubbed his hands together at the sight and his bright beady eyes gleamed. The door was shut and he settled himself down to warm his toes.

He uncorked the bottle, poured a foaming glass full and toasted himself by the firelight. This was going to be a fine night!

The bottle of ale was nearly gone when there came the distant chime of church bells striking midnight. There was the creak of a floorboard behind him. Tommy shot up, peering into the shadowy corners of the room. The ghost shimmered into view. It was a grey figure, dressed in tattered doublet and hose of years before. The old man was stooped and under his arm he carried his own head; swathed in bandages with sunken eyes and a long beard.

'Well, hello Tommy,' the ghost croaked, 'And how are you tonight? Enjoying a winter warmer, I see.'

Tommy tried to hide his shock, replying with mock confidence, 'Oh, it's a fine brew, thank you very much,' and then, 'But, but . . . how did you know my name?'

'That's for me to know and you to find out,' said the head, as the old man shuffled out of the shadows and into the fire's glow.

Tommy could see him more clearly now. There was a scabby wound round his neck where the head had been severed and his ruff was soaked in blood. Tommy took a deep breath. 'How did you get in?' he asked.

'That's for me to know and you to find out!' repeated the voice, as dry as paper.

'Well, you didn't come through the door, that's for sure,' challenged Tommy, his courage rising from somewhere in his shaking body.

'That's for me to know and you to find out,' the ghost sing-songed, a playful smile creasing his face.

Tommy understood the game now. 'Well, did you squeeze through the keyhole? I bet you didn't, only really skilful ghosts can do that!' he ventured.

The ghost snapped, ' Of course I can! How else do you think I get in and out of here?'

'Ahaa,' thought Tommy, 'Now I have him!'

'I don't believe you!' he cried. 'You're just trying to scare me!'

The insulted ghost retorted, 'Of course I can, I can, I can!'

'Well, prove it!' said Tommy, archly. 'I won't believe it till I see with my own eyes. I bet you can't get into this bottle.' He poured the last of the beer into the glass, swallowed it gratefully and set the bottle back down on the table.

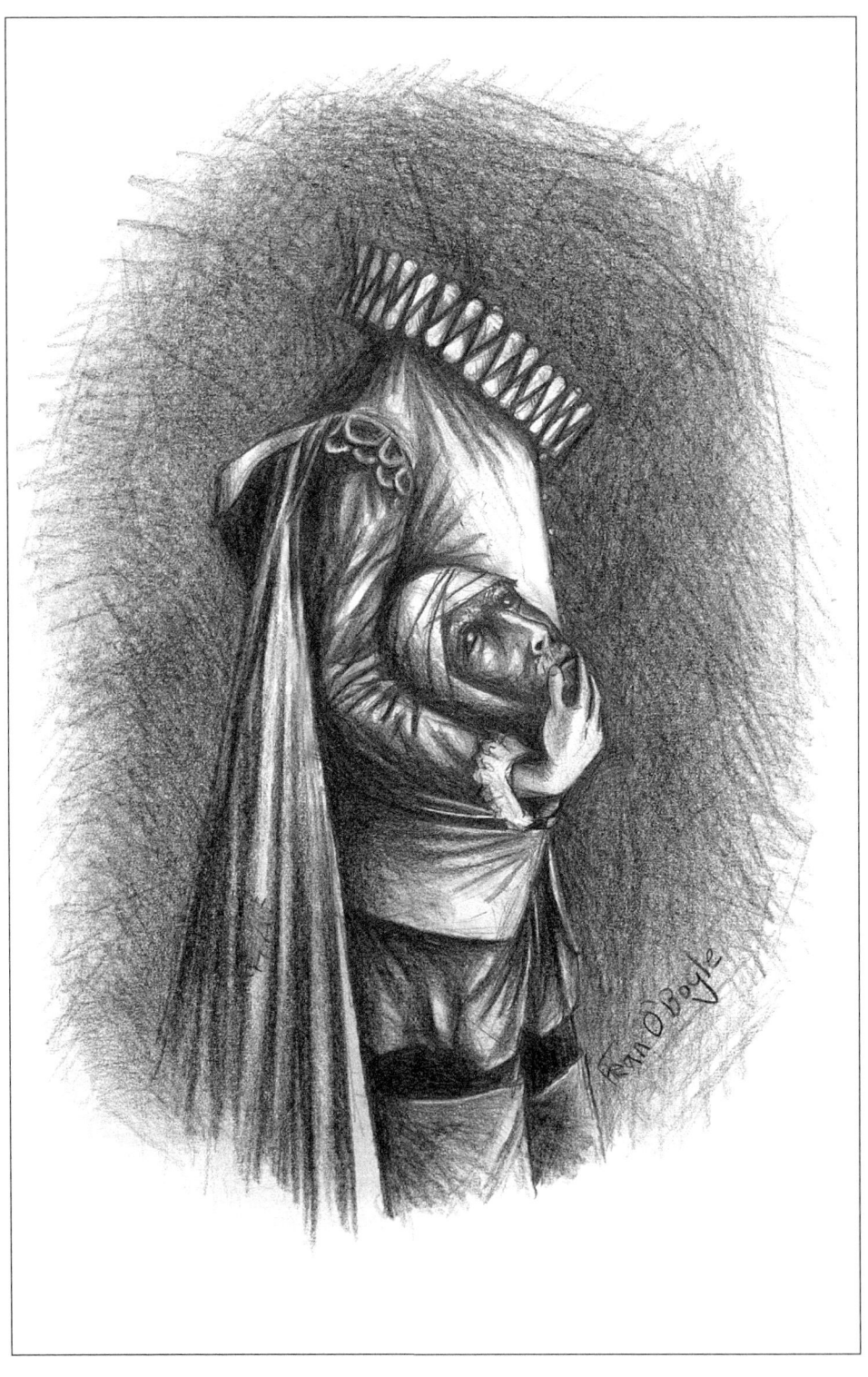

The fire reflected hungry dragons' tongues lapping the sides of the green bottle. Ghost and man faced each other across the table.

'That's the easiest thing to do,' boasted the ghost, childishly. 'Just watch!'

The spectre began to shimmer and as Tommy watched the image became fainter and then twisted and curled into a wisp of smoke. As if it was being sucked, the smoke poured through the neck of the bottle and settled as a tiny grey puff of mist at the bottom.

Tommy leapt forward, pulled the cork out of his pocket and stopped the bottle up as tight as he could.

He flung open the bedroom door and half fell, half ran down the dark staircase and out of the door. Under the bright haloed moon, he scuttled through the icy streets, his footsteps ringing on the cobbles until he came to Ludford Bridge. Positioning himself carefully over the keystone, he flung the bottle into the river.

The house and the town were free of the ghost from that night on. Tommy's reputation as a hero was established and he never went short of a drink right up until he was an old, old man – regaling anyone who would listen with that very tale.

There is a warning that goes with this story, and it goes like this. Should you be picnicking on the banks of the River Teme, or dangling your feet in the cool waters at Ludford Bridge and an old green bottle floats up to you, don't be tempted to open it! You just might unleash a very old, very gruesome and very, very bad-tempered spirit on the town again.

VENGEFUL SPIRITS

Why do ghosts appear at all? Very often such wrongs were committed in their lives that they simply can't rest till they have had their say or tried to put them right. Some characters were so forceful in their living that even death won't keep them quiet!

The first story in this section is a very old ghost story which I have brought up to date by setting it in a modern context and using modern references. As a storyteller sharing and swapping stories with young people in schools and youth clubs, I find there's a type of tale very popular with younger and very active storytellers. They get called urban myths and they are often very old tales, told as recent events, often with a bloodthirsty and high horror content. The main character is sometimes the friend of a friend, which adds to the terror that this story might have really happened to someone still living!

For the Love of Horses

There was once a boy, let's call him Sam for the sake of getting the story told. The thing he loved more than anything else was horses. He loved their power, speed and beauty. At weekends and during school holidays, he was always to be found helping out at the local stables and riding school, mucking out and cleaning tack in return for the chance to feel the freedom and excitement of a canter over the hills.

He came from a large family and his mother and father were constantly reminding him that there was barely enough money to fill the hungry bellies of his brothers and sisters, let alone to take on the expense of buying and maintaining a horse.

So Sam tried all the ways he could think of to earn money to save up to buy his own horse. He dreamt of his own house with a paddock, a smart stable and two or three gleaming horses grazing in the fresh air. But paper rounds and car washing only pay so much and before long he had left school and the world of real work was calling to him.

A local undertaker had connections with the stables where Sam helped out. From time to time a horse-drawn hearse was required and the stables hired their horses for the job. The undertaker had seen how keenly Sam worked and offered him a traineeship in his funeral parlour. The money wasn't bad and Sam could still save up while he did the job. Now and again there would be the occasional horse-drawn funeral that Sam could help out with.

Time passed and Sam grew to be a fine assistant. He was unperturbed by the cadavers, becoming a skilful embalmer and sympathetic to grieving families. Still he yearned for his own horse. Saving up was so slow and the routine of work gave him less and less free time to be a stablehand and get out on the hills on horseback.

One day, the body of an old lady, Mrs Fitzherbert, came into the parlour. She was a wealthy local woman, known to be a mean and miserable recluse. Her sour-faced daughter was overseeing the funeral arrangements.

'My mother is to be buried wearing the diamond necklace my father gave her,' she requested. So on the day of the funeral and under the watchful eye of the daughter, Sam placed the diamond necklace around the corpse's neck as she lay in the coffin. The daughter also ensured the lid was securely fastened before the procession departed. Mrs Fitzherbert was buried on a drab afternoon, mourned by a handful of people sheltering under umbrellas from the persistent drizzle.

That night, as Sam lay in bed, he couldn't get the sight of that body out of his mind. Those glittering diamonds were so vibrant and beautiful and seemed at odds with the lifeless corpse. The jewels had potential, their value was wasted underground. Just what could they buy? A car, a house, a horse, two horses, a stable, a paddock?

Sam couldn't let those treasures lie; he couldn't see the chance to fulfil his ambition pass him by. He resolved to take the diamonds. No one would ever know . . . would they? So, in the depths of that moonless night, he grabbed a tool bag from the garage and stole down to the graveyard.

Taking a shovel from the gravedigger's shed at the back of the church, he began to heave the wet earth from Mrs Fitzherbert's new grave. The dirt was heavy with rain and each shovelful weighed a ton. Although the rain fell and a chill wind blew, the sweat poured down Sam's face and neck as he toiled. Suddenly – crack! – the shovel hit the lid of the coffin. With his bare and blistered hands, Sam scraped away the remaining dirt. He took a nail bar from the tool bag and prised open the lid of the coffin.

By the orange glow of a distant streetlight, he saw the ghastly face of Mrs Fitzherbert, her mouth fixed forever in a thin grimace contrasted by the beauty of the sparkling diamonds. Her body was rigid and wedged into the box, Sam struggled to unfasten the necklace. He began to panic. This had taken long enough. Somebody was bound to come and find him if he didn't work quickly. He had to get that necklace, somehow.

He took a saw from the toolbag and hacked away at the neck. It was a clean cut to remove the head, no blood – a good job of embalming. The head was heavy as he held it in his hands and slipped the necklace over the top of the neck. He stuffed the diamonds into his pocket, replaced the head, crashed the lid down onto the coffin, and hurriedly shovelled the earth back into the gaping hole.

When he finished, no one would ever have guessed that the grave had been disturbed since the burial. He was careful to replace the few wreaths in their original position. As the first light of dawn stained the sky, Sam slipped back home to bed.

The next day he packed a bag and ran away from home to London. He was going to start up again where no one would suspect the origins of his fortune. He sold the necklace for a good price at a city jewellers. In no time at all, he had bought a house, lands and stable in Shropshire, somewhere near Montford Bridge. The day finally came for the delivery of his horses. He had picked two, a beautiful bay mare and a strong young colt. They were his pride and joy.

The mare was steady and bright and a good hunter, they rode together well. Yet there was something nervous and jumpy about the colt. Sam had to work hard to handle the beast and their relationship was more of a struggle between horse and rider rather than the easy harmony that Sam felt with his mare.

One day, he decided to take the colt for a gallop over the hills. Sam thought that a good long hack could cement a bond between them once and for all. But the horse was uneasy. As they rode, it pulled and tossed its head. They crested a hill and the colt suddenly began to try to throw Sam off, as if he could bear the weight of him no longer. Sam lost hold of the reins and grabbed on to the horse's neck. The creature whinneyed and cried at Sam's touch. Maybe he was injured, wondered Sam. He parted the fur of horse's coat and noticed an unmistakable red scar, circling the beast's neck. It was hot and swollen. Sam gasped, he had never noticed that mark before.

With guilt like a huge heavy stone that settled in the middle of his chest, Sam recalled the night he had hacked off old Mrs Fitzherbert's head. The sparkle of those diamonds had been as bright as the colt's eyes were now.

A pain settled right over his heart, crushing him, squeezing him tighter and tighter. Sam struggled for breath. The pain was searing through his entire body. The horse gave one last buck of his back legs and threw Sam to the ground.

The horse's eyes were fixed on Sam as he fell to the floor begging forgiveness from God, clutching at his chest. He lay there staring up into the hard, dispassionate eyes of the colt. Sam was discovered hours later by his stablehand, dead with his eyes open; and the colt was never found again.

Squire Blount

Tragedy plagued the household of Squire Blount who lived at the old Hall in Kinlet. He and his wife had five children. Two of them died in infancy, one was mauled by a wild dog and another choked to death on a piece of apple.

The squire was determined that his only surviving daughter, Dorothy, would marry well and do the family proud. Eligible suitors were sought out and introduced to the girl but she wasn't interested in any of them.

Instead, Dorothy had fallen in love with one her father's page boys. They would meet in secret in the grounds of the hall and even in the house itself, when the squire was out on business.

As time went on they got more daring. The lad would pass secret love notes to his sweetheart, concealed under her dinner plate, hidden in her sewing basket and slipped into her hand as he helped her into the carriage. She would smirk and pass shy smiles back to her young man, right under her father's nose!

The page even took to turning away some of the young men invited to visit the hall. He would tell them that her ladyship wasn't home. The dejected young suitors would then retreat down the driveway, still clutching their flowers, peering over their shoulders at the sound of the stifled sniggers of the lady and her love.

The squire suspected the liaison all along but he was unable to expose their relationship. They were very skilful in their concealment of the affair. He died, a sad man; still devastated by the deaths of his children and angry that his daughter remained a spinster.

Squire Blount's funeral was soon followed by the marriage of Dorothy and the page. There was no happier man in Shropshire that day, for the young man gained not only a beautiful wife but also the titles and wealth of the old squire.

As the guests were seated for the sumptuous wedding breakfast, the door of the dining hall flew open and in raced a ghostly procession of four white horses and a coach. The ghost of the squire himself was sat high on the drivers' box, cracking the whip and shouting and bellowing his rage and disgust at the match. The procession rode straight up the middle of the table, scattering both guests and feast.

The squire's spirit continued to punish the couple. Each time there was a celebration of a family birth or banquet in honour of the couple, he would burst into the room driving his coach and horses right through. He was determined that his daughter and her husband should have no peace.

There were accounts of women washing clothes down by Blount's Pool on peaceful summer days. The ghastly carriage and thundering horses, bearing the squire incoherent with rage and anger, would emerge from the waters and career off along the bank and into the distance.

Priests assembled to pray and exorcise the raucous spirit. The squire was eventually 'bottled'. In Kinlet church, hidden away in a corner somewhere, there is the dusty, flat green bottle where he supposedly rests.

Eventually the Old Hall was demolished and rebuilt, some say in an attempt to rid them of the ghost, but the story still lingers on!

The Deeds & Nasty End of Judge Leighton

Squire Leighton of Plaish Hall was known as a greedy landlord, a ruthless judge at Shrewsbury courts and a man with an appetite for the finer things in life. He liked nothing better than to entertain guests at the hall, showing off the treasures and fine architecture that his wealth and status afforded him.

One day, a builder was brought before Judge Leighton accused of a terrible crime. The punishment should have been death by hanging but when Judge Leighton found out that this man was a builder of splendid chimneys, an idea came into his greedy head.

He offered the builder a pardon if he would rebuild the chimneys at Plaish Hall. Leighton wanted them to be the tallest, grandest and fanciest around – a real talking point. So the commission was negotiated and the builder literally worked for his life. For the next weeks, months and years, the staff working at the hall and passers-by would hear the tuneful whistling of the builder grateful for his reprieve. He put his back into his work and toiled to make a stack of ornate and elaborate chimneys. Soon the sound of his merry whistling became well known thereabouts and caused people to spot and listen and then marvel at the beautiful work in progress.

When they were completed the cheating judge promptly ordered the re-arrest of the builder. The man was dragged screaming and struggling and

hanged there from one of the very chimneys he had built, as the judge looked on, smiling that there was now no way that his chimneys could be copied.

The ghost of the builder gave Judge Leighton no rest. He would walk the rooftops of Plaish Hall by night shrieking and moaning.

Judge Leighton continued his ostentatious life, as if nothing had happened. He pretended to his fine friends never to have seen the crazed spirit who would stalk the corridors and landings of Plaish Hall. But dark shadows under the judge's eyes and an even shorter temper than before betrayed the sleepless hell that his life had become.

One Sunday evening, he invited a couple of clergymen for a game of cards. It was as if the wind knew they were up to no good. It gave them no peace as it rattled the windows and whistled through the draughty old house.

They were seated round a table; bottles were uncorked and cards were shuffled. Before the game began, Judge Leighton got up and went to lock the door, lest they be interrupted and discovered. No sooner had he returned to the table, than the great door swung open letting in a blast of icy wind. The judge took the great key from his pocket and locked and bolted the door fast.

The first hand of cards was dealt. Suddenly there was the sound of sliding bolts and a grinding of the lock and again the door swung open. It flapped and crashed on its hinges, great gusts scattering the cards. The wind became hotter and hotter.

A sudden scorching blast of foul-smelling air sent the men cowering under the table and all the lamps and candles went out. In the darkness, the terrified men heard a mighty roar.

Judge Leighton struggled to relight a lamp and in its pale glow the men saw that standing on the table, with his shining hooves, swishing red tail and gleaming black horns, stood the Old Gentleman – the Devil himself.

The Devil threw back his head and laughed. He rapped his toasting fork three times on the table to summon a musician. In came the ghostly form of the builder, who stood in the doorway, clasped his hands behind his back and began to whistle a tune. The song he whistled was simple and infectious, reminiscent of the happy tunes he had whistled as he built the fine chimneys all those years before.

The Devil began to dance. As his cloven hooves stamped, sparks flew up, burning and singeing the onlookers' beards. The Devil's dance got wilder and wilder and the sulphurous wind and the 'flick-flack' of the swirling playing cards added to the tune the chimney builder whistled.

At intervals he would drag one of the terrified men up onto the table and command him to 'Dance! Dance!' At last, the priests and Judge Leighton were there, jigging away on the tabletop. It was as if their feet were enchanted, they were unable to stop themselves dancing. Puffing and gasping for breath they danced as they had never done before.

While the dance got faster they begged for mercy and the wooden table began to smoulder and smoke. The heat of it was scorching the soles of their feet. Suddenly the table burst into flames and the spell was broken.

The wind stopped, the cards scattered to the floor and the men jumped clear of the blazing table and scarpered into the night. All except one. Judge Leighton. He was left, fixed to the spot with fear.

He was never seen again, dead or alive. When morning came and the priests plucked up the courage to go back to the hall all they found on the floor was a stain of blood in the shape of a human body. No matter how hard people tried, that bloodstain could not be washed away.

Successive residents and visitors to the hall have described how sometimes a ghostly troop of horses thunders through the house at midnight, devilishly shrieking as if searching for someone to take the place of Judge Leighton to continue the dance!

As if to add credence to this tale, when building work was carried out on the house early last century, the skeleton of a hanged man, complete with a noose around his neck, was discovered in one of the chimneys. The sad remains were taken away and given a proper burial in a nearby graveyard.

CHILDREN

Cruelty and harm to children is a common motif in folk stories; Hansel and Gretel are abducted by the witch and Red Riding Hood has to escape the dastardly wolf. Ghostly children are mischievous and tragic characters who evoke an extra measure of terror and sadness as we hear their tales.

There is a thought that the story of Babes in the Wood has origins in Shropshire. Two children were found murdered and buried in shallow graves in a wood that acquired the name Babbinswood (or babbies' wood). Time and retelling has shaped a fairytale where they fall asleep in the wood, but it may be that there is a darker, more murderous foundation to this gentler story.

The Tale of Sarah Hoggins

There was once a miller's daughter called Sarah Hoggins. Born into a humble working family, Sarah spent her childhood dressing up as a princess and her youth dreaming of leaving the mill behind and becoming a fine lady. One day, a well-spoken, bright and good-looking young man called John Jones came to work for her father. Sarah took a shine to him, and although he was a simple labourer he was decent enough and she decided to settle for him, and marriage plans were made.

Shortly before their wedding, John took Sarah aside and explained that he had to confess something to her. His real name was Henry Cecil MP and he had already got a wife who had left him for the love of a churchman! He had come to Shropshire to escape the scandal and to live in peace. He revealed to Sarah that he had indeed a tidy fortune kept in a bank in London.

Far from being disappointed, Sarah was delighted to have found a rich gentleman. Henry divorced his wife and he and Sarah travelled to London for a proper society wedding.

A few years later, news came that Henry's uncle had died and Henry and Sarah were now the Earl and Countess of Exeter. It was a real life fairytale, from miller's daughter to lady of the court! She mixed in noble circles, she lived in a fine mansion, and was truly happy with her husband.

Tragically, she died, shortly after giving birth to their fourth son, Thomas. The plaintive cries of her baby still echo round Burleigh Hall at night, calling for his mother who died when she was so happy and so young.

Madam Pigott

Squire Pigott who lived at the grand mansion house at Chetwynd took himself a wife. He was a harsh and uncaring husband who simply required an heir to his wealth and estates. The wife he took was a lady of sufficient pedigree to be the mother of the child but there was no real love in their marriage. Shortly after the wedding, the squire left his wife to rattle round the great house while he departed to London 'on business'. There he caroused the nights away with all sorts of dubious 'ladies' and 'companions'. He would return now and then just to put in an appearance back home.

His poor, neglected wife stayed behind to run the house and yearned for some true love and affection from her husband. In due course, Madam Pigott fell pregnant. She was sickly and frail throughout and spent much of the time in bed; alone and unloved and growing bitter towards her husband.

The birth was not easy. Madame Pigott had little strength and the midwife began to fear for both the lives of the mother and baby. She summoned the help of a doctor.

Squire Pigott was impatiently pacing up and down outside the delivery room, awaiting the news of the arrival of a son. The doctor emerged from the room to explain that he was unable to save both the lives of his wife and the baby. The squire was required to choose.

It took the cold-hearted squire only seconds to declare that the doctor should, 'lop the root to save the branch'. On hearing that her husband willed her death, Madame Pigott cursed him before gasping her last breath. The child died too.

From that day on, her restless, angry spirit continued to haunt the area. It was said that a wisp of white smoke would appear from the skylight in the roof of the Old Rectory at Chetwynd, and would descend on the breeze until it came to rest on the moonlit lawn in front of the house where it would take a ghostly woman's form. Weeping with eternal grief, she clutched a tightly swaddled infant. The spirit would walk through the grounds of the house and along the dark, high-banked lane that went up Cheney Hill.

The betrayed Madame Pigott would sit on the twisted roots of an old tree, combing the hair of her ghostly baby in the moonlight and crying with heart-wrenching sadness. People wouldn't dare go up there after dark, fearful of encountering the moaning spirit.

If a rider were to come past, especially someone racing for the midwife for his own wife, Madame Pigott would jump up in the saddle behind him and clasp her hands around the horseman's waist. She would try to pull the terrified rider down and cling on no matter how the rider tried to shake her off. Her spirit was unable to cross water, and so when they came to a stream she would let go and leave the terrified man to speed on into the dark.

Her ghost was so troublesome in the neighbourhood that twelve churchmen assembled to lay the ghost to peace by reading psalms. The spirit was strong and fearsome and would not be calmed. Exhausted by the effort of such intense prayer, all but one of the clergymen gave up. It was Mr Foy of Edgmond who continued reading psalm after psalm, sweating and becoming delirious with fatigue. The prayers worked, the ghost's power diminished and it shrunk to the size of a mouse, which was then trapped in a bottle and thrown into Chetwynd Pool.

The villagers had a brief interlude of peace. The ghost was at rest under the water.

One day, in the middle of winter, old Mr Foy died. A thick snow and ice had been lying for weeks and on that same day, a child was skating on Chetwynd Pool and broke the ice and the glass bottle that was floating just below the surface. The spirit was unleashed once more!

This time, Madame Pigott was even more frantic than ever. She would jump on to passing wagons and carts, and cling onto carriages. Once again, the required twelve priests assembled, candles were lit and prayers were read good and hard. The spirit flew about in a wild frenzy, snuffing out all the candles bar one. Despite the gloom, the eldest priest urged his colleagues to continue. If that last candle were to extinguish, then the powers of evil would take hold and the Devil and his army of ghosts would come marching in to assist Madam Pigott in dashing them to bits. At last, the spirit began to shrink and move closer to the mouth of the bottle. They continued to pray that spirit into the bottle and corked it good and fast.

This time the bottle containing Madam Pigott's spirit was thrown into the Red Sea so as not to risk any reappearance! Even to this day, Cheyney Hill is also known as Madam Pigott's Hill. At the foot of the hill there is an ash tree, which sometimes shakes its leaves even when there is no breeze. People say this is Madam Pigott's spirit passing by. So long as she's passing through, that's all right. . . .

MURDERS

The story of Bluebeard or Mr Fox is told the world over; a charming man who lures young girls to grim deaths! The story is made complete by a moralising quote taken from the Ingoldsby Legends, *an old collection of stories, imaginings and the source for this one!*

Bloody Jack
of Shrewsbury

This is a chilling tale that happened a very long time ago. Imagine, if you can, a time when the inhabitants of Shrewsbury numbered somewhere around a thousand in total and the castle as we now know it didn't even exist. Yes, that long ago!

Where Shrewsbury Castle now stands, there used to be a wooden watchtower, kept by a man called Jack Bloundell, or Bloody Jack as he became known.

Jack was devastatingly handsome and proud of his good looks and his success in charming women. On moonlit nights, he would walk local girls along the banks of the River Severn. He would spout poetry and declaim her beauty to the stars. The girl would be entranced by the gentility of this man, with his sparkling eyes and blue-black beard.

Jack would take a ring from his pocket and fall down on one knee and propose marriage. The girl would think that all her dreams had come true.

He would then suggest that they go closer to the water's edge, to peer at the moon's reflection. He would lead the girl through the long grass to a standing rock. There she would be murdered: drowned or her throat tidily slit by Jack's gleaming pocketknife. He took great care not to damage the body.

By now, the rest of the town would be asleep, maybe a few folk had been roused by the cries of the girl and, in their drowsiness, mistaken her screams for fighting cats. Under the cover of night, Jack would drag the corpse back home for butchering. He sorted the body parts into boxes and drawers until, by sunrise, his grisly deeds would be neatly packed away until the next full moon; when Jack would go out seducing again.

One such conquest was a local girl called Fanny. She was an unremarkable child from a large family and so relished the attention Jack gave her. One evening he suggested a walk by the river, Fanny accepted and sneaked out of the family house when her day's jobs were done.

It was Fanny's older sister Mary Ann who noticed that her younger sister was gone and an uncomfortable feeling compelled Mary Ann to check up on her. She knew of her sister's love affair but there was something about Jack that gave her the creeps. These were strange times in the town: a few young women had gone missing and a mood of mistrust reigned.

Mary Ann made her way to Jack's tower. He and Fanny were still out walking along the river and so she had the place to herself. Mary Ann shivered as she pushed open the door and crossed the threshold.

Bright shafts of moonlight were breaking through the windows illuminating wooden boxes everywhere, some used as tables or chairs, some stacked one on top of the other, and all were sealed tight. Some were big and others small, lined up side by side, meticulously ordered . . . sorted . . . arranged. As she ran her hands over the carvings on some of the lids, Mary Ann felt a cold shudder run down her spine again.

Pulling her shawl around her, she went up to the loft, where she poked about some more. Again more boxes and crates; some long and thin, others square and stout. Oh, the smell that filled the place. Mary Ann breathed through her mouth to avoid the foul stench of Jack's tower.

Finally, she came to an intricately crafted merchant's chest with about fifty little drawers, with tiny bone handles. Mary ran her fingers over the drawers, she was sure that the handles looked as though they had been made of teeth!

Mary Ann slowly opened one of these narrow, wooden drawers. She gasped. Inside it was a finger! She opened the next and there was another slender finger and another and another, here a thumb, there a ring finger! Mary Ann opened about twenty of the drawers and they all contained an assortment of women's fingers.

She understood instantly what the rest of the surrounding boxes and trunks contained. It was not her fear and unease that had been choking her, but the stench of rotting flesh!

Her terror was interrupted by noises in the yard below. She tiptoed to the window. Jack's figure came into view. He was dragging something behind him, some sort of wet package. A woman's body! He pulled the lifeless shape along by the hair and Mary Ann recognised the bedraggled clothes as Fanny's!

Weeping tears of fear and horror, she hid behind a box as she heard Jack fling the door open. He grunted and cursed, dragging Fanny's body up the stairs, where he stood still. He sniffed the air and scanned the gloomy chamber with his beady eyes. He knew someone was around; he could smell a fresh woman.

There was silence. Mary Ann held her breath and then Jack, still in his killing frenzy, staggered a few steps forward and began to search, growling,

> Come out! Come out ! Don't hide like a rat!
> Come out! Come out! And face Bloody Jack!

Mary Ann seized her moment and pushed at the stack of boxes in front of her. With a mighty crash it toppled over and the heavy boxes scattered, pinning Jack to the floor. Their fall forced some of the lids open and Mary shrieked as severed arms and legs tumbled out. Pale arms clutched at Jack's throat and assorted legs and feet tangled him as he struggled to free himself. It was as if the body parts were trying to hold Jack back, so that Mary Ann could flee down the steps and out of the tower to get help.

That night Bloody Jack was caught. He was tried and hanged for his catalogue of despicable crimes and cruelties. His body was dismembered, his fingers and thumbs were shared out among trophy-hunters, his eyes were taken by a doctor and his head stuck on a pole on Wyle Cop.

It was felt only decent and proper that the remains of Bloody Jack's victims should be buried, so the severed fingers were removed from the chest of drawers and buried. The following spring, shoots were observed coming up from the ground and they grew into potatoes – known as the Lady's Finger variety!

Jack's tower was pulled down and sometime later William the Conqueror began the building of Shrewsbury Castle.

The story lives on and so does the ghost of 'Bloudie Jacke'. Women walking past Shrewsbury Castle have felt their coats being tugged by some invisible force. Some have said that on dark nights they have seen the shapes of a man and a terrified woman struggling at one of the small doors at the side of the castle.

> And now for the moral I'd fain
> Bloudie Jack
> That young ladies should draw from my pen
> It's don't take these flights
> Upon moon shiny nights
> With gay harum-scarum young men
> Down a glen
> You really can't trust one in ten!
>
> Let them think of your terrible Tower
> Bloudie Jack
> And don't let them liberties take
> Whether maidens or spouses
> In bachelors' houses
> Or, sometime or another, they'll make a mistake
> And loose more than a Shrewsberrie cake.

From the *Ingoldsby Legends*

INDELIBLE BLOODSTAINS

In the same way that restless spirits haunt a place because their earthly business remains unfinished, so the evidence of guilty wrongdoings can linger.
In numerous stories that can take the form of an indelible bloodstain. Many of these exist. At Hogstow Hall there is said to be an indelible bloodstain where a man called Scarlett was wrongly accused of murdering a nun who worked there. People have reported seeing a little white ghostly dog, Scarlett's faithful companion, who loyally guards the scene of the treachery in his master's honour. As houses get refurbished, old floorboards replaced, it is vital to keep knowledge of these bloodstains alive in the stories we tell.

The Bloodstain at Condover Hall

During the reign of Henry VIII, the owner of Condover Hall was Sir Roland Kynvett. The hall had been a gift to him from the king himself. Kynvett had an ambitious and ruthless son, Harry, who would stop at nothing to achieve his goals. He wanted rid of his father so that he could have the hall, its lands and wealth to himself.

One dawn, as his father lay sleeping, Harry crept into his bedroom, clutching a dagger. Sir Roland awoke feeling the chill of the blade against his throat and gasped at the glint of the knife.

Before Sir Roland could call for help, the young man stabbed him and ran. Kynvett tumbled from his bed and staggered along the landing and down the staircase, leaving a trail of blood and calling desperately for help. His wounds were severe and he was discovered moments later by his trusted butler, John Viam, dead in a pool of blood at the foot of the stairs.

Harry, pretending to be wakened by the cries, raced down the stairs and promptly accused Viam of the murder. He invented a story that Viam had intended to rob and kill his father and flee the hall that morning. Indeed, when these accusations were investigated, a hoard of moneybags was found in Viam's room, planted there earlier by the cunning Sir Harry.

The wretched matter was brought to trial at Shrewsbury. Throughout the trial Viam protested his innocence. 'I was a good and faithful servant,' he declared, 'Do you want the blood of an innocent man on your hands?'

Harry had power and influence, and a trail of evidence he had planted meant that the unfortunate Viam was sentenced to hang.

On the appointed day, a crowd assembled beneath a dreary sky and Viam was dragged out to the gallows platform. Sir Harry looked on with an expression of smug self-righteousness as the rope was put around Viam's neck and he was granted a last word.

'I pray for misfortune and catastrophe for all successive heirs to Condover Hall,' Viam raged bitterly, knowing how Harry had manipulated the entire affair.

A short time after, a keen local lawyer called Thomas Owen comes into the story. As the son of a Shrewsbury draper, he took an interest in cases involving his home town, and had cause one day to look through the notes of the trial of Kynvett vs Viam. Owen was acquainted with rumours of the boastful and ruthless personality of Sir Harry Kynvett and he had also heard about the dubiously brief period of mourning he had observed after his father's death. Owen's suspicions were thoroughly aroused as he read the details and he vowed to take action.

He found a case for perjury against Sir Harry Kynvett and applied for a licence from Queen Elizabeth I to retry the matter.

Permission was granted and the case was the talk of the town. Everyone had an opinion, so it seemed; Harry's upper-class friends and acquaintances saw him as a rightful heir and grieving son. The lower-class masses saw him as an out-and-out rogue who had abused a servant for his own greedy ends. So passionately did the townsfolk feel the matter that they began to protest, angry crowds gathered and disorder threatened the streets of Shrewsbury.

Queen Elizabeth I was on a progress across the country and made a change to her plans to visit Shrewsbury and so divert attention from the matter.

Progresses were slow-moving, regal affairs and such a journey would take weeks to plan and complete, so before the queen arrived, the retrial had taken place. Sir Harry Kynvett was finally found guilty and hanged. Supporters abandoned their cause and saw him for the wicked man he was. The queen rewarded Thomas Owen with the land and titles to Condover.

However, John Viam's dying curse was fulfilled. One night, shortly after taking up residence, Owen was retiring for bed when the ghost of Sir Roland, dripping blood, crossed the landing in front of him. The ghost must have mistook Owen for Sir Harry and it lunged towards him. Owen backed away, tripped, fell down the same staircase and was found dead the following morning. Owen hadn't even lived long enough to collect the first year's rents from his new estate.

It was said that disaster and misfortune plagued all heirs to the hall from then on and a ghostly bloodstain remained, trailing all the way down the staircase and on to the floor of Condover Hall. No matter how hard housekeepers scrubbed at this stain, it would reappear time after time as a ghostly reminder of the tragic deaths and wrongdoings of this story.

THE DEVIL

The Devil is an important character in stories. He is the personification of evil and features widely in folktales in areas where the church and chapel had an important role. There are many stories the world over of the Devil and his antics and many places are named after him.

The largest of all the rocks on the Stiperstones ridge is known as the Devil's Chair. In a popular tale told hereabout, the Devil seems to have acquired giant proportions and he bore a grudge against the goodness of the people of Shrewsbury. He decided to dam up the River Severn and was carrying stones in a leather apron to flood the town out. The apron strings snapped under the weight of the stones. They scattered across the hill top and are now known as the Stiperstones. The biggest is the Devil's Chair itself, shrouded in mist when the Old Man is in residence. The stones that rolled down the hillside went into a valley, known as Hell's Gutter.

It is said that the Devil sits there and holds court with all the ghosts and ghouls of Shropshire on the longest night when they elect a leader for the coming year.

Slashrags
& the Devil

There was once a travelling tailor who went by the name of Slashrags. He would travel far and wide plying his trade. It was just as well he did, for he was a wily conman, and could never visit the same place twice in too much of a hurry.

He would set up shop in the back room of a local pub and word would quickly go round that the tailor was about. Many a desperate housewife would scrape together the pennies to send her husband off to be fitted for a new suit, sparing her the shame of seeing him trudge off to chapel every Sunday with a well-patched jacket on his work-weary back.

Slashrags would ensure that his clients drank plenty of ale and that the confusion and high spirits of a good night in the pub reigned. Then, with a flourish of the tape-measure, a scribbling of numbers and many a thoughtful shake of the head, Slashrags would make great ceremony of measuring up the queue of men in their long-johns. A bill would be calculated for each customer, with extras added for pockets, reinforced seams and knees and discounts for cash up front. The befuddled customer would part with his money on the promise of the suit arriving by post within the fortnight.

Later, Slashrags would slip out of the pub in the dead of night, with his pockets jingling and a spring in his step. In due course, he would dispatch the suit, but the seams would be merely glued together, the poor cloth badly cut and, despite the great charade of measuring-up, Slashrags only had one suit pattern and size.

The following weekend, the chapel would be full of shame-faced men with trousers up round their calves and waistcoats stretched to bursting across their bellies. Pinched-faced wives would be sitting next to them, bitterly muttering about 'waste of money', 'alehouse bravado' and praying that it wouldn't rain and dissolve the glue.

On one such occasion, Slashrags set up in the Miners Arms pub at The Bog, near the Stiperstones. He rubbed his hands, sure that this was going to be a lucrative visit for he was in mining country, inhabited by chapel-going people who all wanted to look their best on Sundays.

Trade was brisk and Slashrags soon had a queue snaking out of the pub door. It was nearly midnight when he mounted his trusty horse for the road home down through Shelve.

He was riding in wild country, far from any house and he felt the proximity of something unknown. Presently, he noticed a figure standing in the road ahead of him. Someone was waiting. His horse slowed and began to shy from the figure, so Slashrags dismounted and walked towards the man.

'Have I missed the measuring?' the stranger asked Slashrags, 'It's a pity if I have because I wanted to order a suit from you.' Now although the night was cold and Slashrags had a long journey ahead of him, he always had time to strike a deal.

He whipped out his tape-measure and a scrap of paper and began the well-rehearsed routine of measuring up. The customer was particular about the cut, the cloth and the stitching and Slashrags assured him of his best attention, for after all, wasn't he going to pay the best price?

Slashrags knelt down to measure the man's inside leg. Suddenly, he dropped the tape-measure to the ground and gasped. His confident chit-chat dissolved into fearful gibbering.

The stranger had no feet, just a set of red, cloven hooves which steamed gently on the cool of the road. Swishing around, wafting an unmistakable sulphurous stink, was a red pointed tail.

Slashrags looked up into the face of Old Nick, the Devil himself as he removed his hat with a flourish to reveal a pair of sharp horns glinting in the moonlight.

The Devil relished the terror he read in Slashrags' face and he began to laugh, offered the tailor a hand and brought him up to standing.

'I like your style, you rogue,' declared the Devil smoothly. 'I've been watching you operate for a while. Now you can come and work for me. I need some good swindling skills down in Hell and maybe I can get you to make me some proper clothes.' Slashrags tried to run but found his feet rooted to the spot.

'No! No! Don't take me away!' he spluttered and there and then he began to plead for his life and fell to his knees once more.

The Devil was enjoying the desperation of a pleading man, who was weeping pathetically, 'Very well,' said the Devil, 'Let's strike a bargain.' (As well as fine clothes, the Devil loves a chance to bargain — especially if he feels sure he'll win anyway.)

'You make me a suit that fits. Each and every stitch must be exactly the same length and there must be no more and no less than 1,000 stitches. If you can do this, then I'll let you go free. Should I find the stitches are uneven, too many or too few, and if I even smell the merest hint of glue, then I shall invite you to accompany a few of my newest friends.'

At this point, he stopped speaking, and produced a fine leather wallet from his inside pocket, opening it just a crack. Slashrags whimpered as he heard the cries and screams of the souls that the Devil had gathered in there that night, waiting to be carried off to Hell.

'Meet me in a week. Same time, same place,' smiled the Devil calmly, replacing the wallet with a pat and walking off into the dark night.

Slashrags made his way home as fast as he could. He woke his long-suffering wife and explained to her his predicament.

'You made a bargain with the Devil?' she spluttered incredulously. 'Well, you're just going to have to honour it.'

In the calm of the following day, as Slashrags began cutting out the Devil's suit, she advised him to go to the local parson, confess his bad ways and seek his help.

Slashrags began to sew the suit. It had been a good while since he had even threaded a needle! His wife had counted out 1,000 beans and he tirelessly popped one bean in a pot for each stitch.

That night, red-eyed from concentration, he sought the guidance of the reverend, Mr Brewster, and confessed all his years of wrongdoings. Brewster forgave him and advised Slashrags to make the suit, but only with 999 stitches, to deliberately disobey the Devil. The parson also agreed to come along with Slashrags to his diabolical rendezvous in a week's time.

The suit was finished and the night came. It was a fine work. His wife wrapped it in brown paper and late that evening Slashrags and Brewster set off.

Slashrags quaked and trembled, stuttered and gibbered all along the road, but the good Brewster kept driving him on. In the distance, they heard a church clock chime midnight. As the sound faded, they rounded the last bend in the road and there, leaning against a wall, was the Devil. He brandished a newly sharpened toasting fork, which he nonchalantly spun in the air like a cheerleader's baton.

Brewster dived over the wall leaving the terrified Slashrags to go on alone and meet his fate. Slashrags silently held the parcel up towards the Devil who smirked, put down his toasting fork and tore at the paper.

'I hope you remembered the 1,000 stitches, Slashrags?' he teased. Then the Devil suddenly stopped. He could hear the intense mumbling of prayers from the other side of the wall. The sounds of the good words recited by the parson were like scalding oil being poured into his ears.

'Stop that noise! Stop it now!' roared the Devil, clasping his manicured hands to his ears. But the prayers were fine and the sound managed to wriggle round his fingers and drip like syrup into his head. The Devil began to scream in agony at the kindness of the psalms. He could bear it no longer and instantly disappeared into the night in a red cloud of stinking smoke, leaving Slashrags standing, open-mouthed.

From that time on, Slashrags was a reformed character. There was no finer, more honest and hardworking tailor and maker of parsons' vestments in the whole of Shropshire. The toasting fork that the Devil left behind was kept in his family for generations, but nobody ever used it for making toast. The bread was always tinged with a sulphurous taste that no sweet jam could ever mask.

Will o' the Wisp

Will was a hardworking blacksmith, who lived a humble life in Shropshire. He had three loves: his life, his family and their home. And since he had all of those three things, you could say he was one of the happiest men around.

One evening, he was tidying up his tools and looking forward to a night by the fire where he loved to dandle his youngest son on his knee, while telling stories to the older ones. He was just about to throw the wooden bolt across the workshop door when a stranger came into the yard leading a horse.

The horse had lost a shoe and the stranger asked Will to fix another one so he could be on his way. Now it was late, Will was tired and hungry and the last thing he really wanted to do was start the furnace up again. However, he could not see a stranger stranded for want of a shoe and so being a good man he fixed the horse up in no time.

There was little conversation between the two men as Will worked, the stranger didn't wish to divulge his business and Will was content just to get the job finished.

When the horse was all done, the man lifted the hood from his cape to reveal a head of glistening golden hair that shone in the moonlight. He told Will that he was no other than St Peter himself who had come down to earth on God's business. In return for his kindness, St Peter granted Will one wish.

Will had most everything he could want; a contented life, his needs well met and an easy conscience. There! He had it now! How would it be to live without a rested secure heart? What would it be like to make different choices, to choose the reckless path when all Will had ever known was the honourable one? He wondered and then he spoke.

'I wish,' said Will, 'That I could live my life all over again.'

The wish was granted and Will found himself being reborn in an instant. He grew up and lived his life all over again. Only this time, he took a very different path. Instead of finding a wife to love, a family to cherish and work to sustain him, he became a gambler and stole money and cattle to pay for the fine wines he developed a taste for. He took himself three or four wives and left each of them with children to feed as he galloped off into the sunset.

He was a chancer, a crook and a rogue. Finally, Will met his end as the loser in a duel of pistols at dawn.

It was no surprise when, after the life he had led, Will found himself at the great wooden doors of Hell. He knocked and a tiny peep-hole window in the door opened and the Devil's bony nose peered out to see who was there. Old Nick took one look, gasped, slid the little door shut and Will could hear the Devil ordering his demons to bring reinforcements.

Will knocked again and waited. The chilly winds that blow between the worlds of the afterlife made Will pull his coat around him as he waited for the Devil to reappear. Finally the door slid open, 'Go away. We don't want you here. You're too wicked even for this place,' snapped the Devil and Will could hear an army of little demons straining as they pushed against the door of Hell to keep it shut, lest he should try to force his way in.

Will turned away from Hell and thought that maybe he should give Heaven a try. So he mounted a staircase which towered up into a speedwell-blue sky, he held onto the golden banister rail and watched little chubby cherubs float by on clouds until he was standing before the glistening gates of Heaven.

Will jingled the bell pull and waited. St Peter opened the pearly gates and as he did so the smells of fresh baking and the sounds of sweet music ushered forth into the chilly no-man's land where Will stood.

St Peter recognised him instantly. 'I gave you a special wish and how foolishly you used it!' scolded St Peter. 'You certainly don't deserve a place here.' He turned away from Will, clicked the gate shut and left him standing on Heaven's doorstep.

Will had no choice but to go back to Hell to see if Old Nick would relent and let him in. He needed somewhere to go! The staircase between Heaven

and Hell was beginning to look familiar as Will trudged down to the great oak-studded door and knocked again.

The Devil reappeared, impatient and scolding. He was adamant that there was no space for Will there and slammed the door in his face again.

Poor Will turned to face the black abyss where he was condemned to wander for evermore. He hunched down in front of Hell's gate and put his face in his hands, and felt the bitter chill of the 'tween worlds down the back of his neck.

All at once, Hell's door opened for a third time and the Devil reached out with a pair of tongs. Clasped in the end of the tongs was a red hot coal fresh from Hell's furnaces, 'Here, take this. It'll keep the chill off,' he said and slammed the door.

Will gratefully tossed the coal from hand to hand, appreciative of the heat, although it burned him. This was the only warmth he was ever going to feel as he walked through the rest of eternity: a glowing coal given to him by the Devil in a single moment of pity.

As you make your way home, late at night, you may come across little pockets of fog that seem to come from nowhere at all. Now, while the scientists have an explanation for these patches, let a storyteller tell you the truth. What you can see is the smoke off the coal that was given to Will who was too wicked for Hell.

You'll never see Will, as he is too ashamed of his last earthly life and the foolish wish he made, but you will see the plume of smoke he leaves in his wake as he walks the earth forever with nowhere else to go. We call this smoke Will o' the Wisp, and now you know why!

This is a story told the world over which is presented in the book Shropshire Folklore, *gathered by two Victorian ladies, Charlotte Burne and Georgina Jackson. Indeed their volume, which gathers stories, rhymes, superstitions, sayings and songs, is an important collection for anyone interested in finding out some of the older folklore of Shropshire. In her commentary about this story Charlotte states that to the best of her knowledge the tale of Will o' the Wisp is a German tale, but was told to her by a Shropshire lady. It just goes to show how stories can travel and be adopted by a storyteller and reared as their own.*

It is a delightful tale, and as a frequent traveller around the Shropshire lanes I am sure I have met Will on Shropshire soil, as maybe others have too.

OTHER MALIGN & MAGICAL CREATURES

As well as the Devil, Shropshire has its fair share of fairies and other creatures from the other world. Fairies are not always sweet creatures, flittering about playfully on gossamer wings. They have a more earthy connection to us mortals and move among us, unknown and in disguise, to dispense justice, punishments and cruel mischief.

The Legend of Ogo's Hole

Near Llanymynech in the side of the hill is a hole. It is the entrance to a cave and network of tunnels beyond. It was believed that the fairies lived here and sometimes you could find odd gold coins scattered on the ground outside, which was said to be dropped fairy treasure.

There was once a fiddler who travelled in these parts between weddings and celebrations, he was much in demand for his music. Nobody quite knew how he did it, but his tunes were so infectious and his playing so lively that even the tiredest legs were hard pushed to rest when he swirled up a tune!

Blind Ned Pugh, for that was how he was known, made his way along the lonely lanes feeling his way with his stick and with his fiddle strapped to his back. He was a man of few words: it was as if the fiddle did the talking for him. He was solitary and silent – and kept a deep secret.

Ned had once been sighted and a hardworking farm labourer. In each quiet moment, young Ned would steal away and practise tunes and dances on his fiddle, by the flickering firelight late into the night at the back of the grain store when there was a lull in the work.

One evening, as he played away to himself, a little fairy man came out of the shadows and sat listening awhile. Ned looked up and saw a little man with a crooked nose and spindly legs who had appeared out of nowhere. He thought he'd seen a ghost and, trembling with fear, he dropped his bow and the room was filled with hush.

'Don't be afraid, young Ned,' the fairy soothed, 'I've been a-listening to your tunes for a while now and I've come to ask you a favour and offer you a gift.'

Not realising he was now talking to a fairy, Ned listened as the little chap asked him to come and play at a wedding the following Saturday night. Ned was to meet him at the crossroads where he would be taken to the party to accompany the dancing.

Flattered by the offer, Ned agreed. A deal was struck. 'So what's the gift?', he enquired.

'The gift of music fast and sweet
To fill rooms and hearts and make busy feet!' chanted the fairy man.

He raised his stick and instantly Ned's fingers began to whisk up and down the fingerboard, the bow flew through the air and the sweetest music filled the room. Ned smiled and chuckled as he played. He was no longer struggling to pick out a tune in slow practice; instead, jig after reel after waltz after polka flowed, fast and accurate. The fairy man receded into the shadows, leaving Ned playing long into the night.

The following Saturday night came, and the fairy kingdom was a-buzz with the excitement of a party. The tables were laid with food, the bride and groom glittered in gold robes and the cave was festooned with fresh flowers. The disappointment was bitter when Ned didn't show!

Of course he didn't; he was busy playing away in one of the local pubs! Ned was now very much in demand, applauded for his new talents, and showered with coins and praise. Ned wore a smile as wide as the English Bridge in Shrewsbury! He was so busy relishing his new skills and basking in his fame that he had completely forgotten the bargain he had struck with the little man.

Later that evening, or earlier the following morning, Ned was making his way home along a quiet lane. His ears were still ringing with cries of 'More! More!' from the adoring dancers and his pockets were heavy with the money he'd collected. Out of the shadows stepped a silhouette, with a familiar bony nose and spindly legs.

The fairy man blocked Ned's way, his face was dark with anger and gone was the mischievous sparkle in his eyes. He raised his stick and pointed it at Ned, and uttered a slow curse:

> 'Skill you have, not ta'en way
> But you shall not see the joy from this very day!'

Ned felt a searing pain in his head and he fell to the floor. When he awoke, he felt the warmth of the sun on his body but could not see. He had been blinded. He retained the skill of music in his fingers, but just as the fairy had promised, he was unable to see the delight it brought to people's faces and feet.

From that day on, Ned lived his lonely life, travelling the road, tap-tapping with his stick, bringing joy with his music, but always brooding silently on his treachery that had paid him back so bitterly.

One night, as Ned walked back from a session, he decided to take a short cut across the heath. The night was bitter and the wind was raw. Nobody quite knows what happened: he could have just sought shelter in the entrance to Ogo's Hole, or maybe he entered the maze of tunnels beyond to find the fairies to apologise, but Ned was never seen again.

Into Ogo's Hole he went never to re-emerge. Lost underground forever.

Some believe that the faries took him prisoner, glad when he finally showed up to play for them after so many years. Even when he died, the fairies resurrected his ghost to play music for them at their command. You can indeed sit in one of the pubs in Llanymynech and hear faint wisps of music seeping up through the floorboards now and again as Ned fiddles away for eternity as the fairies dance.

A similar story is told on Clee Hill, where a young gypsy girl is lured into a cave by the sound of sweet music and stumbles across a fairy party. There she spots a relation of hers, imprisoned by the fairies and condemned to play music there forever more. Nowadays, we are all like the fairies, keeping music prisoner in our CD collections and MP3 players!

Many, many years ago the belief in household fairies was alive. Brownies were helpful and good creatures to have around. People would even leave out dishes of porridge for them. Bogies were bad goblins and every bit as terrifying as a ghost, plaguing people with menaces and bad luck. Contrast the two types of household spirit in these next stories; the industrious brownie and the idle bogie.

The Welsh Brownie

Mr Nicols hired a young Welshman at the spring fair to work for him at Yockleton Park. He was industrious, strong and eager to lend his hand to all tasks. Mr Nicols was pleased and the farm profited well, partly because of the Welsh lad's efforts.

He was so pleased that he threw a Christmas party with plenty of meat, cake and ale. The whole house joined in the revels until there was a loud hammering at the door and a clanking of chains in the yard outside. This was not the sound of someone wanting to join in the party but the noise of malice and harm.

The ladies hid their faces in their skirts and in one anothers' arms, and the children clutched at their mothers and screamed in terror for the noise was loud and fierce. Mr Nicols bolted the doors back and front and placed himself bodily in front of it when the Welshman volunteered to go and investigate the noise.

Nicols insisted that the Welshman should not go out into the dark and the two men's angry exchange of words became blows. Young and strong as he was the Welshman overpowered Nicols, threw open the bolts and went out into the noise and terror of the night. He was never seen again. Mr Nicols left the lad's wage packet out on the table where it remained, untouched, for a whole year – maybe it paid for the cake and ale at the following year's Christmas party!

The family concluded that the lad had been a willing drudging goblin, a brownie. He had done his time with Nicols and under the cover of that mystical interlude between Christmas and Twelfth Night, when the curtains between this world and the magical realms are lifted, he was claimed back by his own kind.

The Gorsty Bank Bogies

Just south of Callow Hill is Gorsty Bank. There was once a farm there that was beset by two bogies; a little wizened old man and his revolting wife. With beady eyes, dripping noses and hairy chins they were each as fat and smelly as the other.

At night, when Farmer Reynolds and his wife had gone to bed, they would sneak out of the shadows and warm themselves by the embers of fire, tearing at the bread dough left to rise and souring the milk for breakfast. The family would be wakened in the middle of the night by the sounds of pots and pans clattering and smashing as the pair had a right old time of it. By day, they would torment the lambing ewes, blunt the tools and steal the hens' eggs.

The Reynolds family was desperate to be rid of the old couple, who clung like fat leeches onto the hospitality they stole. They had called in the priest to read prayers and holy verses to rid them of this torment, but the pot-bellied little bogie-man and his wife just sat in the rafters, swung their legs and cackled with raucous laughter at the priest's endeavours.

Finally, the family decided that there was nothing more to be done; they simply had to leave the farm. The whole move was plotted and planned in whispers, so the bogies would not discover their plan and follow. In stealth, the house was packed up, their belongings loaded onto a cart and one afternoon while the bogies slept off a fat feed of beastings (the first milk of the newly calved cow) in the stable, the family took off.

As they unpacked the cart, at the other end, Mrs Reynolds noticed that her favourite salt box was missing. Carved by her grandfather, it was precious

and about the only treasure the family possessed. Edward, the cowman, was instructed to sneak back to the old house and retrieve the box for them.

As Edward retraced their steps along the road, imagine his shock when he saw, coming towards him the little pair of bogies with broad grins on their faces; between them they were carrying the salt box!

'You forgot your salt box,' grinned the old man, 'So we thought we'd bring it along with us. Aren't you glad?'

Dumbstruck at the barefaced nerve of the pair, Edward walked back along the road with the bogies, dreading what his master would say when they all turned up.

The family must have seen them walking up the farm path for by the time they reached the door they kept whatever annoyance they felt well concealed. Instead, they were most hospitable to the little old man and his scritch-scratching wife. Mrs Reynolds invited them in and gave them some food and drink in the kitchen, while Mr Reynolds and Edward busied themselves in the barn outside.

The men piled up sticks and logs to make a great roaring fire at the open end of the barn and then the farmer got Edward to lie on the ground while he covered him in straw. Presently Mrs Reynolds showed the bogies into the barn on a conducted tour of the new house.

'And here's where you'll be sleeping,' she smiled pleasantly and the little man and his wife made approving noises.

'Aw, very nice, very nice indeed,' they clucked, looking around at their new surroundings, arms folded across their ample bellies.

'And as you can see,' she went on. 'My husband has lit you a nice fire to make you feel at home. Please take a seat and warm yourselves,' she urged and bade the couple sit on the hump of straw under which Edward hid.

As soon as the bogie and his wife sat down, Edward jumped up and tossed the little fat couple into the roaring fire. The straw sparked and blazed and Mr and Mrs Reynolds each grabbed a pitchfork and held the couple down. They howled and screeched and begged for mercy before being swallowed up by the dancing flames.

The fire put an end to that scavenging couple good and proper, leaving the Reynolds family in peace and prosperity.

HEROES

The Romans began the mining work which has influenced the landscape in south Shropshire and affected local life ever since. It has continued to shape the landscape above and below ground. Underneath the Stiperstones hills are a maze of tunnels and mineshafts which were once perilous to unwary walkers and attractive to children for playing in. They are now fenced and gated. Many locals still relate stories of having played in these deserted mine workings and levels.

Wild Edric

Tales are told about Wild Edric, who was a Saxon chieftain. Edric lives on in the Shropshire imagination as two very different characters; a tragic man, heartbroken and bereft and also as a hero awaiting his time to come and save the county. Maybe all men have an element of both in their characters.

One story goes that, while hunting in the forest one day, Edric and his band of men heard music playing and followed its sound into a misty clearing. Dancing in the dappled sunlight was a ring of beautiful women. One of them had hair like spun gold and a smile to rival the brightest of sunbeams. To cut a long story short, Edric fell madly in love with her there and then. As if in a trance, he approached the woman and fell at her feet, vowing his undying love. She revealed herself as Godda, the Queen of the Fairies, and introduced the other dancers as her sisters. She promised to marry Edric only on the understanding that she would need to disappear once in every while to meet her sisters and dance. She also made him pledge never to speak to her in anger.

Edric was ready to promise anything and so they were married and lived as the happiest couple ever there was in Shropshire. Time went on, Edric living his warrior life, returning to bask in the glory of his wife's smile and Godda disappearing to the woods from time to time and returning renewed and refreshed.

One day Edric had been out on a long hunting trip. The weather had been harsh and the sport was poor; he returned home in a bad temper, wanting

the comfort of his wife. He searched for her in the house until a servant girl explained that she had gone to the woods. He waited impatiently for her return.

After some time, the door burst open and in came Godda, eyes wild and hair tangled with twigs and leaves, knees and cheeks smudged with mud. Edric rose from his seat and bellowed, 'I needed you and you weren't here! Where have you been? Gallivanting with your sisters in the woods, I suppose!'

Godda stopped in her stride, put her head on one side and enquired, 'Are you cross, Edric? Are you raising your voice to me in anger? Well then, you shall see me no more.' She turned on her heels and walked out of their home and Edric's life forever.

Stories tell how Edric rides across the South Shropshire hills at night, eyes streaked with tears, tormented with the desire to find his wife. He cries, 'Godda! Godda!' at the top of his voice. As you lie in bed, you could confuse the sound for the wind whistling round the eaves of the house – but listen carefully. When the wind dies down, you will hear the gasps and grief-wracked sobs of a man destined to live for eternity with regret.

Edric also lives in Shropshire folklore as a bold warrior and a saviour. He is supposed to sleep under the Stiperstones Hills, concealed in the maze of tunnels and mine workings, waiting for his moment to return for battle.

Many locals can recall playing in the adits and tunnels as children, taking torches and exploring for miles underground. There was a young lad, Davy, and his mate playing in the entrance to a mine working where they had played many a time before. On this particular day, their game took them further into the level, where the air was cold and the passage narrowed to a tight squeeze. The one boy was scared and turned back. Undaunted, Davy pressed on, driven by the curiosity of his young mind.

The squeeze opened out into a huge underground cavern. As he shone his torch around, it caught the glint of metal. Davy looked harder and saw a pile of treasure spilling out of sacks and bags piled against the cave walls. There was a veritable hoard of golden plates and dishes, coins and gems.

With the sound of the steady drip, drip of water from the roof echoing in his ears, he continued to shine his torch around.

The beam landed on the gleam of a saddle buckle and flash of a silver stirrup and Davy saw that the treasure was guarded by a group of warriors. There were about eight of them, mounted on strong horses and all of them heavily armed with axes, swords and shields. They were all sleeping deeply. Davy now realised it was the sounds of their snoring which he had mistaken for the sound of the wind eddying around the cavern.

The statue-like figures were still but for the gentle rise and fall of their sleeping shoulders. In the middle there was one figure, most heavily armed and mounted astride a magnificent armoured stallion; this was clearly the Edric of the legends Davy had been told.

Davy saw his chance and reached forwards to grab a handful of gems and quietly prise away a goblet from the tottering pile of treasure. As he did, a coin tinkled to the ground. The bright sound roused one of the sleeping men. A blonde, tousled-haired man woke and rubbed the sleep of a hundred years from his eyes. He stretched and in a gravelly voice, thick with a century's dozing, cried out, 'Is it time, Edric? Shall we go into battle now?' When none of the other warriors stirred, Davy thought quickly. 'No! no!' Davy blurted, 'Sleep on, my friend, it's not time yet!' The blonde warrior closed his eyes, rested his head back on the hilt of his sword and instantly resumed his deep, snoring sleep.

Davy clutched the treasures he had managed to steal and tiptoed out of the cave and along the level back to daylight.

Despite the best efforts of local mining historians and underground explorers, nobody has found Davy's cavern and Edric's treasure. The story goes that the ghost of Edric rides out on the eve of major conflicts and he can be heard thundering along the lonely lanes around the Stiperstones, roused by the impending crisis.

WATER

The idea of a water spirit dragging you in occurs time and time again as a motif in the stories we tell. Trolls lurk under bridges ready to grab billy goats, and ponds are said to be inhabited by Jenny Greenteeth – a water witch whose strands of green hair float on the surface.

Shropshire is cut through by the River Severn and with its flooding and ever-present power it renders the fear of water and terror of drowning very real, even in a land-locked county.

Ancient beliefs in water spirits that protect valuable water supplies and wells mutate over time, and when these spirits begin to acquire characters and form they start to inhabit the folktales as nasty forces or magical mer creatures.

The Asrai

There was once a poor fisherman who lived by the shore of Ellesmere. Although he worked each and every day that God sent, it never seemed enough, and so to try to make ends meet he also took to working on full moon nights too.

One such night, he cast his dragnets over the side of the boat and sat looking at the moon's reflection. It glistened on the water like a silver penny. The fisherman smiled. If only all the moons he had seen were really silver pennies, then he could catch them in his nets and be a very rich man indeed. But those riches would only ever exist in the sky, like the pie he was never able to set on the table to feed his family.

With a deep sigh, he came out of his reverie and reached to haul in his net. The weight of it this time was tremendous. He hadn't felt it so heavy for many a trip. He heaved and pulled excitedly. There was a great catch in it, for sure.

He tumbled the net onto deck and began to rake through the contents. There, among the weed, he noticed an arm, a pale and slender limb. As the fisherman pulled back the net he saw that he had caught something that looked like a small child. Beautiful and finely boned and alive!

As the fisherman gazed into the wide fearful eyes of the child, he knew instantly that he had caught an Asrai. Such is the name given to water spirits that inhabit the dark murky depths of meres and lakes. With their water-weed hair and webby fingers and toes they live unseen, undisturbed in chilly peace, at the very bottom of the water. It is said that once every hundred years, on a full moon night, they come up to the surface of the water to peer at the

moon and it is that glimpse of the silvery light that enables them to grow, just a little, each time. So while this Asrai looked about twelve years old, she may well have been ancient.

The fisherman spoke soothingly to the Asrai, assuring her that he meant no harm. He fancied taking her home and showing her off to his children: what a feast for their eyes when they woke up!

The Asrai began to chatter and gabble to the fisherman, in a voice that bubbled, sighed and sucked like water at the lake's edge. It was unintelligible to the man, except for its pleading tone. Over and over again, she pointed at the bright moon.

As he watched the desperate creature, the fisherman then had a better idea. Maybe the moon had brought his fortune that night after all! He would row as fast as he could to the great lord's house nearby and sell the creature for a bag of silver. His lordship could display the unusual pet in his fishpond!

With his mind set on the prospect of new wealth and his heart bursting with effort, he rowed on, not listening to the plaintive cries of the Asrai imploring him in her strange language.

The little creature wriggled and squirmed on the deck of the boat. As she freed herself from the net, she reached up to grab the fisherman's arm.

The touch of the Asrai made them both recoil. To the fisherman, it was as if a shard of ice had burnt his skin, so deep and intense was the chill. For the Asrai, the warmth of a human body was so strange that she shrank back and cowered with fear on the deck of the boat.

As the first signs of sunrise began to taint the distant sky, the water spirit covered herself with her slimy hair and huddled into a tiny ball. The fisherman recognised that the sun might dry the creature and so he ripped up a handful of wet reeds to cover her body as he continued to row the length of the lake.

He landed the boat and jumped out to drag it a little way up the stone beach. Then he reached over to lift the reeds away from the little creature and saw that there was nothing there, just a wet patch where it had been cowering. The creature from the watery depths had vanished at the slightest glimmer of sunlight.

From that night on, his arm bore a red scar from the Asrai's touch and he had a frozen patch there for the rest of his life, which he would explain away with this story.

The Nicky Nicky Nye

Once there was a man who decided to go and look for a wife. It was going to be no easy task to find a woman who would come and make her home in his lonely cottage in the wood. So he decided to go looking where nobody would know of him or where exactly he lived. One day, with his dog at heel, he went through the heart of the wood and out the other side on his quest.

He walked and walked until he came to the outskirts of a village where he had never been before. There was a stream running below the road, where a beautiful young woman was rinsing clothes. He watched her as she worked. She had golden hair that sparkled in the sun and the bluest of eyes. He fell instantly in love: never had he seen such a girl.

He leant on a wall and asked a farmer who was working in the fields about her. 'Oh, you don't want to get messing round with her. She's known as Lizzie Luck, but she'll bring you nowt but trouble,' cautioned the farmer.

'Ah, but she's awfully pretty to look at,' said the man, 'I reckon I could forgive anything of a girl with those eyes.'

'She's a scold, with all sorts of airs and graces,' replied the farmer. 'She and her mother are poor and penniless, but she still reckons she's sommat special. Take my advice and leave well alone,' warned the farmer.

His words fell on deaf ears as the lovestruck man strode down to the riverside where the girl was working. He lifted her up by the arm and promptly marched her off to her mother's house to get permission to marry her. It seems that was the way it was done in those days!

The mother couldn't believe her luck and neither could the girl. They thought that with her notorious bad temper she would be a spinster forever. So, with her pinny still wet from washing, the three of them, accompanied by the farmer as a witness, set off to find a priest, and they were married by teatime!

The girl barely had time for a quick goodbye to her mother before the man took his new wife by the arm and set off home again.

'But what about my clothes and my things?' protested the girl.

'You've no need for them where we are going,' said the man. 'Time enough for new dresses and pretty bits and bobs when you've proved yourself a good little wife!'

The girl was furious at this. But his grip on her hand was firm and she was unfamiliar with this path that led through the woods. If she ran away now, she would be lost, so she could do nothing but go with him.

The man's trusty spaniel trotted along at their side, every so often showing its teeth and growling at the young girl.

Their nearest neighbour in the wood was a wise old woman known as White Mary. Nearly bent double over her stick, she was always muttering strange rhymes and incantations to herself as she pottered around the tangled copse in which she lived, collecting herbs and brewing up remedies and potions. They had to pass by her house on their way home.

'Come and see my new wife, Mary,' the man boasted loudly.

All was silent. Mary didn't come out; instead, the door was opened a crack and Mary threw out a bunch of lucky wild flowers and herbs. It landed at Lizzie's feet. The young woman began to rage. Here she was, standing in a bedraggled dress, in the middle of nowhere, with a stranger for a husband, on what was supposed to be her happiest day. Now, to cap it all, her only wedding present was a bunch of old weeds. She picked up the flowers and tore them up, scattering them on the ground. Her new husband scolded her not to be so ungrateful and the dog began to snap and bark at Lizzie, jumping up and trying to bite her.

Sniffing and snivelling, she carried on her way, feeling utterly miserable and casting sideways glances at the snarling dog which walked at her husband's heel. She wondered how she was ever going to live with this hard-hearted man and his spiteful, snapping dog.

Presently they neared the cottage and crossed a bridge over a stream that ran in front of the house. 'Now,' growled the man, 'If you know what's best for you, mind your meddling ways. I don't want you moving or changing anything around in my house, do you understand? And whatever you do, don't ever go near the brook, for Nicky Nicky Nye is waiting there for you.'

He took her to peer into the clear twinkling water that ran under the bridge. Suddenly she let out a scream. She saw something! Two green eyes were looking up out of the water. Green and scaly, it was Nicky Nicky Nye alright; an evil water spirit who lurked under the bridge.

That was why the man lived a lonely life. People were afraid to visit and cross the bridge, lest Nicky Nicky Nye's cold clammy arms reached up, grabbed them and dragged them into the water.

The next day the husband went off into the woods, leaving Lizzie about the house. She went out into the garden looking for a space to plant a parsley bed and found that the garden was curiously ringed with ugly stones.

'We've no need for them, they take up too much space,' she tutted, throwing about three or four over the hedge into the stream. She began digging the soil ready for planting.

Suddenly she stopped work. She realised that she had disobeyed her husband's warning and had altered the garden. Maybe she should retrieve the stones? But that would mean crossing the bridge and wasn't Nicky Nicky Nye waiting? Hadn't she seen his eyes?

She decided to leave it be. After all, it was only a few stones.

That night, as the couple sat by the fire, they heard noises outside the window; jeering, laughing and sing-song taunts. They got louder and louder. Somebody was dancing in the garden. The dogs began to whimper and pace the floor. The husband rose and Lizzie froze to her seat.

'What have you been meddling with?' he roared.

'I only shifted three stones to make a parsley bed,' she stammered.

The taunts and sneers outside the house reached a wailing pitch. The husband unbarred the door and let the dogs out. The laughter changed into shrieks and screams and was heard retreating into the distance. When the dogs returned, her husband reminded her not to interfere with how things were arranged in the house. That night, Lizzie slept uneasily; starting at the slightest rustle of leaves or sleepy whimper of the dogs.

A few nights later it was a full moon and the husband went off hunting. She begged him not to leave her alone with Nicky Nicky Nye so close by.

'Now let the other night be a lesson not to meddle with the things you dunna understand!', he instructed. 'From now on, be sure to stay clear of the shady places, only go outside where it's bright sunlight. You've left a gap for him to squeeze through and he's watching you.'

'Can't White Mary come and sit with me? I'm so afraid,' implored Lizzie.

'What! After the way you spoilt her wedding gift? She's not wanting anything to do with you,' he exclaimed. So he left the spaniel to guard her and off he went.

Presently, Lizzie went out into the sunshine to get some water from the spring at the bottom of the garden. When she got there it was too shallow to dip the bucket, so she took some odd stones and began to build a little wall to allow the water to collect.

The spaniel stood at her feet growling with something like disapproval as she worked.

'Oh! Quit your narky ways!' she cried, spitefully, taking a stone and throwing it at the dog. The stone caught its leg and the poor thing cried out with pain. She took the dog and shut it in the shed with two others that had been left behind, and left it to suffer.

When she returned to her work, she had another sudden realisation of what she had done. She had meddled. By rebuilding the spring she had interfered with the order of things. Fear began to seep through her body.

The ash tree over the spring was tied with ribbons. It was the custom in those days to dress wells and springs to thank them for the water they gave. Lizzie had an idea. If she borrowed the ribbons to tie in her own hair, her husband would be so enraptured by her beauty when he returned that he'd forget to be cross about the little wall she had built around the spring.

She sat in front of the crackling fire, plaiting the red ribbons in her hair ready for her husband's return in the morning. The wind was whipping up outside the house. Then, between the gusts, she heard the thin sound of menacing cackles, sing-song taunts and the sound of fingers scraping at the shutters and scratching the door.

Her heart began to thump in her chest. She was alone. The dogs were locked up outside; she could hear their howls across the yard. She clapped her

hands over her ears. But she couldn't block out the wailing. She ran upstairs to hide under the blankets. As she ran into the bedroom, suddenly a big twiggy hand with long nobbly brown fingers shot through an open window and tired to grab her.

Struggling to slam the shutters fast and fight off the rough, scratchy fingers, she saw that the ash tree was gone from its usual place by the spring. It was scrabbling at the windows as Nicky Nicky Nye danced and sang around the garden. The tree wanted its ribbons back and Nicky Nicky Nye wanted her!

She managed to clap the shutters closed and hid under the bed listening to the storm of menaces that raged outside. Presently, there was the sound of dogs barking and growling and the laughter changed to screams as the demons were driven away. The dogs had escaped.

Then there was silence. Lizzie waited a fear-filled while, crept downstairs and opened the door. White Mary was standing on the step. She looked reproachfully at Lizzie as she held the wounded spaniel in her arms as the other dogs paced round her ankles.

She remained by the fireside for the rest of the night, keeping the peace, muttering spells and nursing the wounded dog.

The terror of the night taught Lizzie that the cottage had been carefully ringed with magic to keep evil at bay. Lizzie hated her husband's faithful spaniel who reminded her of her cruelty and not to fiddle and meddle, and of fear of the night when she did.

In time, she fell pregnant. There were no two happier people than that couple when their son was born. They were delighted when he began to smile, then to gurgle and finally, one day, to crawl.

One summer day, Lizzie was pegging out the washing while the baby crawled at her feet and the spaniel dozed in the sunshine. The baby was watching a ladybird and was trying to follow it. Down the garden path he went, with surprising speed and unseen by his mother. He heard the tinkle of the stream, abandoned his ladybird hunt and went to the water's edge and peered in. He was entranced by the babbles and sparkles. Suddenly, two long green arms reached up out of the stream and grabbed the baby into the water.

Lizzie heard a splash and looked up, knowing instantly what had happened. She ran down the path and plunged into the water after her child and began to wrestle with Nicky Nicky Nye for the screaming baby. The demon clutched the baby to its clammy chest and flailed about with its other arm like a cold strand of pond-weed, whipping her across the face and body as she tugged. The dog was roused and jumped in the stream and began to growl and bite.

The spaniel bit hard into Nicky Nicky Nye's green scaly flesh and wouldn't let go. The monster cried and howled but the dog held on tight. As he tried to free himself from the spaniel, Lizzie got the child and herself out of the water and into the arms of her husband who had come running at the noise.

The dog was carried off downstream still clinging on to Nicky Nicky Nye, who was never seen again in those parts. The little dog was gone too. His master was heartbroken at the loss.

In quiet moments, there in the cottage by the stream, the ghost of that little dog would come back time and again. It would pad noiselessly through the open door and sit at Lizzie's side, resting its head on her knee as she sat and nursed her babies. They both made their peace with one another. Lizzie couldn't bear the creature any more malice, and would whisper her eternal thanks to the creature for saving her son and the rest of the family from the terrors of Nicky Nicky Nye.

STORIES OF OUR TIMES

Stories are constantly evolving and changing, tellers adding their own spin to an event, amplifying details for extra effect. Indeed, folklore is being made all around us even today.

The Fires of Wem

On 3 March 1677, a little girl called Jane Churm was poking about in the attic of a house on the corner of Leek Street and High Street in Wem. Nobody knows exactly what she was up to. What we do know is that she had a lighted candle and the roof was made of thatch! The resulting story, which spans three centuries, is certainly worth telling.

Some say that Jane had snuck off to her bedroom up in the gloomy eaves of the house to read under the bedclothes with only a candle to light her book. Others tell how she had been sent up to the attic to collect dry kindling to bank up the fire to dry the washing.

The roof of the house caught fire. Within minutes the blaze was raging through the town. The place was engulfed in smoke and the flames could be seen from miles around licking round the chimney pots. The town was devastated and it was a miracle that only a few cows and a single citizen, a humble shoemaker, perished in the flames. It was soon known that Jane had started the 'Great Fire of Wem'. She was wracked with guilt and could never forgive herself for what she had done. She lived to be an old lady and the torment followed her to her grave.

In 1995, Wem was ablaze again. This fire destroyed the Town Hall. As the smoke rose from the charred embers, which were damp and steaming from the fire-fighters' efforts, a photographer went to document the aftermath. When he developed the pictures, he was stunned to find the faint image of a girl in a cap and petticoat peering round a doorway. Could this have been the

ghost of Jane Churm, come back in her child's form to pick her way through the wreckage of yet another fire in her home town?

The story gets more bizarre. The process of refurbishing and rebuilding the Town Hall began. One thing that had survived the fire was a plaque commemorating the first Great Fire of Wem. It needed to be removed and sent away to be restored and remounted. It was being cut from the remaining plaster on the wall by a couple of men and lowered by block and tackle to the ground. The chain suddenly slipped through one of the builder's hands. It came crashing to the floor and broke the other man's left foot.

The plaque was duly put on a lorry and dispatched to a factory somewhere in the Midlands to be remounted and polished, ready to go back into the new Town Hall. While the plaque was there, the restorer's factory mysteriously caught fire. The small factory was destroyed but the plaque survived that blaze and was eventually remounted and sent back to Wem.

As the delivery van carrying the plaque travelled along the motorway to Shropshire, its engine caught fire! Luckily nobody was hurt, and the plaque was salvaged from the burnt-out van and loaded onto another van to continue its journey.

Finally, back safe and sound in Wem, the builder reattached the plaque to its final resting place on the newly painted walls. The screwdriver slipped, he lost his grip on the plaque, it fell to the floor and landed on his right foot – and broke that one too!

It seems that the ghost of that little girl's guilt from all those years ago still lingers in Wem.

GRAVEYARDS

Graveyards are the ideal setting for ghost stories; shadowy, mournful places where you can be with your thoughts and memories and the spirit of whoever is passing through. St Julian's graveyard in Shrewsbury is said to be haunted by the ghost of a man who died while staying at the Lion Hotel. No one was able to discover any next of kin but a bag of money meant that there was enough cash to cover the costs of a burial. The body was laid to rest in St Julian's churchyard. Over the next few days and nights sounds of cries and groans emanated from the new grave, terrifying passers-by. After three days and nights, permission was granted for the grave to be dug up and investigated. The inside of the coffin lid was covered with scratches. The corpse's hands had no fingernails left and were covered with blood where the 'dead' man had woken from his sleeping sickness to discover that he'd been buried alive!

This fear is played out further in another story which comes from the south of Shropshire.

The Phantom Funeral at Ratlinghope

Nestling on the western flank of the Long Mynd is a small settlement called Ratlinghope. Subject to rogue fogs, snowdrifts and sudden weather changes, this is one of the most isolated communities of south Shropshire.

A long time ago, a traveller was walking towards Ratlinghope. Tall and gaunt, his face told of the hard life he had left behind and his worried brow faced uncertain times ahead. He was heading for the home of a relative with whom he'd arranged to lodge in return for help on the farm. It was a cold night; he pulled his thin coat around him and leant into the bitter wind that was gusting up the valley known as Hell's Gutter.

Suddenly, the wind abated and the traveller stopped in his tracks for he could hear the sound of hooves. As it neared, the traveller guessed that there were maybe four or six horses pulling a carriage. He stepped to the edge of the road to make way, for they were clearly in a hurry.

The sound got louder and louder and he could hear the whinnying of the horses as they were driven fiercely on. A vehicle careered round the corner, illuminated by the moonlight and coach lamps, which burned dimly. It came to a halt as it drew level with him.

The horses stamped and steamed in the bitter air and the traveller looked up at the grey shape of the driver who was staring ahead with glazed, almost unseeing eyes.

The traveller noticed that the horses pulled a flatbed cart upon which there was a coffin. He respectfully removed his hat and wondered at the irreverent speed at which this funeral procession had been galloping along.

Another man dismounted from the cart. He was old and stooped and around his waist he wore a carpenter's apron. With a bony finger, he beckoned the traveller to come closer. Wordlessly he opened the lid of the simple wooden coffin. His eyes were fixed on the young man and a wry smile twisted across his lined face as the traveller peered to see the corpse within.

There was no corpse. The coffin was empty. The joiner-cum-undertaker began to move towards the traveller and took a hammer from his pocket. The young man gasped and understood at once why the ghastly procession had stopped. They were looking for a body to fill the box. His body! He turned to run but the undertaker began to pull and claw at the traveller's clothes.

Although he was exhausted from his walk and weary from the night, the traveller summoned up his last remaining shreds of energy to fight himself free from the hands that tore at him.

The distant chime of midnight church bells broke the chill of the night and announced the arrival of the witching hour. At the sound, the undertaker promptly jumped back onto the cart, the driver cracked the whip and the ghastly procession clattered off down the road, leaving the bewildered traveller scrabbling in the muddy lane.

Desperate, cold and shaking he made his way finally to the farmhouse where he was expected. The farmer's wife warmed the terrified man by the kitchen fire. He was dumb with fear but she didn't need him to explain what had just happened to him.

The ghostly funeral is a common sight around Ratlinghope. Sometimes the procession is calm and reverent and at others it frantically gallops around the lanes and tracks – in frenzied pursuit of a body, any body, to fill the coffin. There are people who claim to have witnessed this ghastly horse-drawn procession to this very day.

Bibliography

Burne, Charlotte S. (ed.), *Shropshire Folklore*, first published Trubner and Co., London, 1883, reprinted EP Publishing Ltd, 1973

Hartshorne, Charles Henry, *Salopia Antiqua*, January 1957

Ingoldsby, Thomas, *Ingoldsby Legends*, www.exclassics.com/ingold/ing40.htm

Ridge, Richard, *Shropshire Highland Folktales*, 1937

Shropshire Magazine, December 1957 and April 1988

'Shropshire Folklore of Yesterday and Today', from *Folklore* Vol. XLIX, Sept 1938, pages 223–43

Tongue, Ruth L., *Forgotten Folktales of the English Counties*, Routledge and Kegan Paul, 1970

Other useful reading

Hughes, Jean, *Shropshire Folklore, Ghosts and Witchcraft*, Wilding & Son Ltd, 1977

Nicolle, Dorothy, *Shropshire Walks with Ghosts and Legends*, Sigma Leisure, 2003

Palmer, Roy, *The Folklore of Shropshire*, Logaston Press, 2004

Rees, Howell, *The Ghosts that Haunt Shrewsbury*, 1995

Other sources

www.mythstories.co.uk

The Morgan Library, Aston Street, Wem